Erotica Sex Stories

Taboo short Lesbian Stories collection for adults. MFM Erotic Women Menage Explicit Forbidden. MFFF Ganged & Shared

Sasha Coleman

COPYRIGHT

This document is geared towards providing exact and reliable information with regard to the topic and issue covered. The publication is sold with the idea that the publisher is not required to render accounting, officially permitted or otherwise qualified services. If advice is necessary, legal or professional, a practiced individual in the profession should be ordered. - From a Declaration of Principles which was accepted and approved equally by a Committee of the American Bar Association and a Committee of Publishers and Associations.

The information herein is offered for informational purposes solely and is universal as so. The presentation of the information is without contract or any type of guarantee assurance.

Contents

In Paradise

I lie there, looking up at the starry sky, which is splendidly spreading out in front of me, and I suddenly realize that at this moment I am probably the happiest person in the world.

So happy that I wonder if I shouldn't have a guilty conscience. A guilty conscience towards people who are not so well off and who may have deserved happiness far more than I do.

Next to me under the sheet is a beautiful, naked girl.

Sara sleeps soundly.

No wonder with the intensity with which we drove it together twice that evening.

Until then, however, it was a rather rocky, sometimes painful way.

It's a slightly longer story and I try to be brief:

it started in a rather dramatic way two and a half years ago. Back then, when I was 20, I took a long vacation on the French Mediterranean island of Corsica after several unpleasant strokes of fate; at least that was how it was planned.

However, after a few days in the southwest of the island, I was involved in a serious car accident. I was able to pull a young woman out of her burning car, but it hit me so badly that I had to stay in the hospital for some time. The young woman's family comes from a very small coastal town in the western part of the island, and since I was still ailing after I was discharged from the hospital, they took me in.

I felt comfortable and at home in this environment from the start, and the people from the village also liked me, which is a miracle when it comes to Corsican attitudes towards strangers. It went so far that they prepared an empty house for me in the small harbor of the village. It was more than just gratitude for saving one of your lives, it was the unspoken mutual agreement that the chemistry between us was right.

To cut a long story short: since that time I have been living and working there, if you like, I have my new center of life there. My circumstances at the time allowed this to happen without any problems. I practically worked my way through the viticulture and the winery quickly because there was an acute shortage of personnel. Otherwise I was able to contribute my technical knowledge, was financially on my own after six months and felt incredibly comfortable in this village community.

The following two years went by in a flash, I learned a lot and enjoyed my life in this unique landscape, together with these great people.

Luckily for me, there was only one missing, and this problem made me more and more troubled.

I was alone.

An ancient biblical wisdom says: It is not a good thing that man is alone.

Plain text: I longed for a female being, for love, for sex, for everything that a man longs for in the early twenties.

The people there were nice and nice, but also manageable in numbers. The only unmarried woman of my age at that time was Marie, whom I had rescued from the car. As a result, she had to postpone her planned wedding to a young man from the neighboring town by two months and did not throw herself at my neck out of sheer gratitude.

The next theoretically possible person was Nicola and, at just under 13, was far out of my reach.

Collette is the good soul of the village. A resolute, firm woman, her husband is a fisherman and the two run a restaurant with genuine Corsican home cooking. Collette is an authority in the village, her knowledge of human beings is almost infallible, her opinion is heard and has weight, which is very unusual for the more patriarchal Corsica.

Back then Collette knew very well what was going on with me and was very worried because she was afraid that sooner or later I would leave the place. But ultimately she couldn't help me either.

Only the many new impressions and the daily learning distracted me. I had to leave the sexual component of my life to my hands, coupled with the threatening knowledge that this cannot be a permanent condition.

And then came the evening of July 23rd, which was supposed to change everything.

And that too was initially an event with a certain drama.

I was driving that evening after dark when I saw what looked like a man in the ditch on the narrow coastal road just before the village. I stopped and found a young woman who at first sight appeared to be unharmed but not really responsive. I quickly packed her in the car and drove her to our druid. We call it a little fluffy. He is a retired doctor who spends his twilight years with us, but takes care of the medical concerns of the villagers when necessary.

I delivered it there, but then I had to continue because I still had a lot to do in the wine cellar. Afterwards I went to the druid again.

He said that everything was ok with her, that she was German, that she was with friends at a nearby campsite and that she had got lost. She has a slight sunstroke, is quite dehydrated, but he has taken care of her, now she is sleeping in his guest room, everything is fine. Your people at the campsite knew I could be reassured.

Somehow I hadn't really noticed who I was picking up. It was dark, although I could see that it was a young woman. But I just wanted to get her into medical care quickly because I was afraid she was seriously at risk

The next morning I had a full program, one of the fishing boats had an electrical fault. I had to deal with this for a few hours.

I came back around eleven o'clock, and then what happened to be called a magical moment happened. And there should be some more of these magical moments.

I went to the kitchen through the outside of the restaurant.

And then Sara stepped out the door.

I know it sounds insanely cheesy now, but I can't change it. Then, out of the blue, this dream of a girl stood before me, and it had happened around me from one second to the next. Almost the size of me, slim, long blonde hair, light blue eyes, a beautiful, clear, friendly face, dressed in a flannel shirt and shorts that were a bit too big, Marie had lent them both.

I stood there in awe of this radiant beauty and didn't know what to say.

If I ever imagined a dream woman in sultry dreams, she looked like Sara.

"You are Mattis?"

".. I ... yes ... oh yes, actually yes Matthias, but here it speaks out unwieldy, the Frenchman Mattis gets off his tongue more easily." I babbled tangled stuff.

We then sat down at a table and she told me her story:

She had graduated from high school in the spring of this year, by the way also had a driving license and was then absolutely ready for a vacation. A friend persuaded her to go camping in Corsica for four weeks with her and six other people she didn't know, which turned out to be a fatal mistake. Three of the six people were solo men who had probably launched an internal competition, and who was the first to succeed in laying Sara down. The constant pursuit and the omnipresent sexist chatter had become unbearable for her after only a few days. And when one of them wanted to do her laundry yesterday morning, she freaked out, kicked him in the balls and then just started running.

She was sometimes very impulsive, she said. Today, where we have come very close in the meantime, I would rather call it highly passionate.

In any case, it would now bring nothing in the world to return to them. She should now urgently try to reach her parents to somehow organize her immediate return to Germany. The booked ferry would only go in three weeks.

At that moment, Collette brought us a drink and asked if everything was okay. I roughly explained what Sara had told me. Then I literally felt her wince and start to work tremendously in her.

And then suddenly in her own resolutity she said to Sara:

"It's out of the question. You stay here. You deserve your rest. We can still get you here, and you get food and drink too."

I had to translate it because the Corsican dialect has only roughly something to do with French. Sara looked at me questioningly and I explained to her:

"The Corsicans are a little different from the Germans. Offers are not made out of politeness or tactics. They mean this seriously and honestly."

And Sara accepted.

It was only later that I understood that Collette meant the offer with absolute honesty, but that there was also a not inconsiderable portion of the calculation.

In the following three weeks I went through hell.

From what Sara told me it was absolutely clear to me:

The girl is taboo for me.

She wants to be calm, no turn on, no advances, just to be friendly with each other. We were together all the time every day, she helped in the wine cellar, went with me to the vineyard very early in the morning, she went with me to the sea, I taught her to dive, I was constantly looking for her near and was equally busy, to keep them at a distance.

I felt like a pubescent confirmation student and had to painfully relearn how cruel it feels to be in love when it seems so hopeless.

What made matters worse by a few potencies was the fact that the apartments on site were all occupied and the druid needed his guest bed for his sister, who wanted to visit for a few weeks. There was nothing left but Sara to stay with me. And I - very gentleman - moved onto the boat. However, that only worked for just under a week, because it was so hot that summer that it became unbearable.

So it happened that we both spent the last of the three weeks in my bedroom, the beds pushed apart as it should be.

It could have been so damn easy if I stupid fool only interpreted the signals that Sara was constantly sending out. She was just like me. She wanted and wanted me to the same extent, but also didn't know what to do with it. The girl was totally unsettled because I didn't start her gentle advances, even though she felt that she was impressed in every way. Every now and then the top buttons of her shirt were opened as if by magic and gave me an insight into the beginnings of her small firm breasts. When we worked together, she took every opportunity to bring me into contact with parts of her body. Her happy laugh was irresistible.

However, I Depp was completely focused on ignoring it and avoiding any attempt to approach it that might be misunderstood.

It was fatal. We were both keen on each other, but neither of us managed to reveal ourselves to the other.

How stupid you can actually be. Rosamunde Pilcher could have written an entire novel from this material.

And then came August 15th, the day of her departure.

It was agreed that I should drive her to Ajaccio at noon, where she could take the booked ferry with the others.

I woke up in the morning and suddenly felt sick. It hurt so much.

Sara was awake before me, and she had made a final effort to somehow resolve this stupid situation. If that didn't work now, I'm just gay or something, it would be like that.

She put everything on one card.

"Tomorrow Mattis .."

"Hello Sara"

"From now on you have your home for yourself again."

"Yes ..." I laughed tortured.

"You Mattis ..."

"Mmmh" I looked over at her. She had turned to me, resting her head on her hand. Her nightgown was again at least a button open.

"I don't know how to thank you. It was a wonderful time here ..."

"Oh Sara, that's fine, don't worry." I stared at the ceiling.

"Well ... I would like so much ..."

Silence ....

Then she gathered all the courage available.

"I'd like to come over to you and give you a kiss, as a thank you."

It was like a stab in the heart. I still hadn't understood the full post. Sara awaited my reaction. And then I let my tormented soul run free.

"You Sara ... please don't ... that wouldn't be a good idea. Please don't get me wrong, but you mean a lot more to me than you think. It's so difficult for me to let you go starting something like that, I would not be able to cope with ... "

And then I pushed out of sheer frustration:

"I'm probably no better than your buddies from the campsite. I just want you to do the laundry. I'm sorry ..."

And then I closed my eyes and waited for her to get up and leave the room so I could could finally start crying. That was exactly what I felt now.

And then she got up.

And then I felt her sit on my bed.

I opened my eyes. Sara was sitting right next to me, looking at me with wet eyes. Then she leaned over me, her hair falling over my face.

And she said very quietly and very slowly:

"You stupid idiot. I don't want to leave, I want to stay here and I want you to do my laundry ..."

And then she kissed me.

I don't know the anatomy of the human brain. But I know there is a region somewhere that controls the release of happiness hormones. And in this region there must have been a full short circuit in this second. That was a little too much: deepest depression, despair, darkness, sadness and then suddenly light, joy, perspective, future from one second to the next. I had fireworks in my head, it popped and flashed in every conceivable color and shape.

I grabbed Sara, felt her warm body push against me for the first time. We laughed and howled and kissed and clung to each other, all at the same time.

I will never forget this indescribable moment of happiness in life.

At some point we broke up, were full of euphoria and didn't know where to put it.

I then ran out to Collette, who was just setting the tables outside. I stood in front of her and just said,

"She's staying ..."

She looked at me completely amazed for a second, and then turned her eyes to the sky, started to cry, called something I didn't understand, and then she hugged me.

Then I suddenly realized that in everything she had been doing recently, she had been working towards what had happened now. The druid's sister was invented. Of course there would have been a bed for Sara somewhere. Collette knew I wouldn't be able to let Sara go. It was clear to her that I would have returned to Germany sooner or later. And she had also registered exactly how much Sara and I wanted each other. Now her plan was working.

I spent the rest of the day in a trance.

At some point Sara and I got into the car and drove to Ajaccio to inform the others that she was not coming. It was a very windy day, it would be stormy on the open sea.

When I met the others, there was an unpleasant incident: The guy Sara had battered her balls with didn't want to accept all of this. First he insulted Sara quite badly, and then he attacked me and threatened me. We hadn't told them I was German, they thought I was a Corsican.

In fact, after two and a half years on the island, I had also internalized some Corsican traits in addition to the language, including a certain pride, and that was just being seriously injured. And I reacted accordingly:

I grabbed his collar, pressed my knee between his legs and nailed him to the quay wall. And then I said a few words in Corsican. If you master it, it sounds so wonderfully martial. Nobody understands it, but it is impressive.

Apparently I came across quite believably, because after that there was silence.

We then waited until everyone was on the track and then made our way back home.

When we were back in the car, Sara wanted to know what I said to the guy.

"No, I'm not telling you that, it was out of anger, I needed that for my own well-being at that moment."

"Come on, tell me, I want to know."

"No, please Sara, I can't possibly say that, it was a bit rough."

"Matthias ... please .."

"Shit ... I just slipped out. I told him that he was a little lousy rat and that if he puked over the reef this afternoon, please remember that I want you to lie flat and flirt at the same time with pleasure ... Please Sara, that was not meant seriously. That was out of affect. "

To my relief, Sara started to laugh out loud.

"Such a shit that he didn't understand that."

We were in an open Suzuki jeep that belongs to the village community, but which I mostly used for all sorts of purposes. We drove along the coast road and I was still carried by this wave of euphoria.

Sara's long blonde hair blew in the wind, our eyes met every now and then and she laughed at me every time. The last twelve hours had turned my entire life upside down.

"Stop there, please."

Sara pointed to a small parking lot surrounded by pine trees. I thought that she had to go for little girls and put the car under a tree. But I was wrong.

As soon as we stood, she undid our two straps, swung her leg over me and sat facing me on my lap. And not only that. She pressed her slim body against me, rubbed her lap on mine and gave me a kiss on the tongue, so that I couldn't breathe.

"What's wrong with you .." she gasped with her mouth open.

"You wanted me to do the laundry. So, what are you waiting for."

That was the last thing she said to me for the next five minutes, after which the only moaning came from her mouth. I was completely surprised. She pressed her torso and lap against me with tremendous intensity, I let my hands slide under her shirt over her bare back. Through her shirt and shirt, I felt her firm breasts rub against me and her lap pressed against my cock, which had developed into a powerful erection in my short in record time. After a while she had to stop her kisses, otherwise she would not have been able to breathe, instead she gasped and moaned in the crook of my neck.

In a brief hint of reason, I risked a quick glance around to make sure we were really alone, but as Sara's activity increased, I didn't care if anyone saw us or not. With growing excitement, the lines between reason and lust become more and more blurred until in the end there is only lust. Sara couldn't have been stopped now anyway. I suddenly felt her whole body cramp, and then she moaned her deep satisfaction in the hot afternoon air.

I was completely stunned. Since this girl had rubbed against me in the middle of a parking lot to orgasm without any warning. For the first time I had an approximate, exciting premonition of what else I can expect with Sara.

I hugged her for a while until she calmed down a bit.

I took her head in my hands and looked into her sweaty flushed face.

"What was that now?"

She was still laughing a little out of breath.

"I don't know either, actually I just wanted to give you a kiss, but then I somehow blew the fuse."

I laughed and hugged her again.

"Do you actually know what you did?"

She broke away from me and looked at me questioningly.

"Why what?"

"You totally sucked my pants."

She moved away from me and looked at my lap, on which she had just rubbed. Indeed, there was a small damp mark left by her own soaked jeans in the crotch.

Sara grinned. "Oh, I guess I lost it a bit, but it's only a small stain with you."

I frowned: "I don't mean the stain on my pants, but the mess in my pants ..."

She looked at me briefly with astonished eyes, and then she started giggling like a little schoolgirl.

"What, did you spray your pants?"

"What's there to laugh about ..." and with a reluctant look in my eyes I added:

"Where else should I have sprayed?"

Then she looked deep into my eyes, put her forehead on mine and then repeated my question very slowly, quietly and deliberately, that it sounded like a promise:

"Yes, where else should you have sprayed?"

For the next time, however, she had to leave it at this exciting promise, because in the evening she got her days, and when they were over, she wanted to wait until she was safe in her contraceptive time, because she lacked our first contraceptive method wanted to enjoy sex together without a condom.

However, this did not prevent us from explaining our bodies to each other in the meantime and learning what others enjoy and enjoy.

But when the time came, Sara made two crucial mistakes:

We had a larger party in the restaurant that evening, and I had been involved in the preparations since early morning. In an unobserved moment, Sara suddenly stood in front of me, put her hand in my waistband, gripped my balls and whispered very softly in my ear that I should prepare myself mentally and morally for the content of what she was holding keep placing where nature intended during the lunch siesta.

I admit that my wording is a bit cumbersome at this point. Sara whispered to me literally:

"This afternoon you can finally inject into me .."

The result was that I was completely under power for the rest of the morning. I couldn't get a clear thought out of sheer anticipation and kept walking around with a more or less pronounced stand, depending on whether she was near me or not.

When we finally lay naked in bed with each other, the second hammer came:

Even slightly breathless, she asked me to act a little gently at the beginning, since - I quote - she was still intact around the bottom.

Sara was still a virgin.

That gave my already tremendous excitement another boost. I registered the first drops of pleasure on my acorn without her or me having even touched it.

And so the catastrophe took its foreseeable course.

The moment when Sara was lying with flying breath, pleading eyes and legs wide apart and with trembling hands and firm grip wanted to lead my rock-hard penis to its warm, moist destination ...

... I came .... violently. ..

And instead of feeling my longed for cock in her belly, this poured a felt liter of hot sperm on her belly.

I can still see Sara's expression right now when I collapsed on her with a loud groan, this mixture of lust, surprise, helplessness and disappointment.

With all the fibers of her body and mind she was focused on the fact that now and in this second my penetrating cock robbed her of virginity ... and then this broke.

So it happened that we had to extend our siesta by one hour that afternoon. After an intermezzo in the shower, we ended up in bed again and brought each other back up to operating temperature. And as stupid as that may sound, but after the pitiful failure in the first attempt, it gave me great satisfaction that on the second attempt I managed to have Sara take off on her defloration according to all the rules of art. And not least due to the fact that I had already released the first pressure, I managed to slowly but steadily fuck the girl to a fulminant and fulfilling orgasm after a necessary careful intro, which was rousing in every respect:

I was allowed to spray a second time, this time not on Sara's stomach, but deep inside him.

After a little rest and refreshment, I went back to the kitchen. It took Sara a little longer with her shaky legs.

Collette's broad grin spoke volumes. Sara had played half the village with her orgiastic cheers. I had forgotten to close the window.

If you limit yourself to sex during the period of non-conception, this means that you have to pull yourself together enormously on the unfavorable days. On the other hand, it increases the desire for each other immensely, so that it can lead to extremely intense and passionate love games.

And we have a very special place for that: Paradise.

Paradise is in a small gorge near the village that the brook from the mountains had dug over the millennia. The center of paradise is a gumpen, a natural water basin that the brook dug into the rock, circular, about six meters in diameter and three meters deep. Right next to it is a kind of cave that Claude set up as a love nest for himself and his then fiance and current wife many years ago. Claude has a locksmith's shop in the village, and he had discovered this wonderful piece of earth by chance at some point, since the only access is only through a narrow crevice, which for safety's sake he had blocked through a massive wooden door against passing tourists. In the open cave he had set up a hotplate and a place to sleep, the waterfall rushes around the corner, macchia and pine trees grow on the edge of the rump, which exuded a wonderfully spicy smell in the hot summer months, on the sides the rock borders this place from the Outside world. From the cave you walk a few steps over a rock slab and jump into the pool.

No wonder that Claude named this heavenly place "paradise".

The absolute sensation there, however, is the floating lawn, which he designed and built for himself and his partner, a truly bold construction. It consists of a three by three meter wooden frame in which a mattress of the appropriate size can be placed. This frame hangs on a canopy and is connected by a chain via a roller to a steel cable that is stretched across the narrow gorge. Usually this frame hovers over the rock slab. If you have made yourself comfortable in it, you can release a locking device on the side, and then, as if by magic, you will hover over gravity following the force of gravity. On hot summer nights there is nothing more relaxing than sleeping a meter above the cool water.

Claude is Marie's father, but even without this connection, we had gotten on incredibly well from the start. Like Collette, he too had noticed from the start that I felt comfortable and committed within our village community. And he was happy as a little child that I was now going to continue this life here with Sara.

Shortly after this totally surprising development, he showed me his paradise and offered to use it whenever I felt like it.

Today I showed Sara this place for the first time. Yesterday's announcement that she wanted to attack me today after days of abstinence from siesta had made me extremely hot. However, I had other plans and I promised her a surprise for the evening.

In the afternoon I went with her on the way. We had logged out for three days. We loaded provisions and the necessary utensils into the car and drove to the entrance to the gorge. Sara had no idea what was going to happen to her, and she was amazed when we squeezed through the narrow wooden door with all our luggage. Behind the door it went up steeply over roughly hewn steps, and then the view of paradise opened up, to our paradise.

Sara was speechless.

It was incredibly hot, but here near the waterfall the heat was bearable, there was that typical, spicy, Corsican scent in the air, the birds chirping, the sun shining through the pine trees. It was fantastic.

I showed Sara the cave with the bed and the cooking area and of course the large lawn. I had been here briefly in the morning and had prepared everything.

Now Sara stood on the edge of the pool, lost in thought.

I literally felt what was going on in her head, the same thing that was going on in my head. We still hadn't fully processed the events of the past few weeks because it was so incredibly much that was falling on us and also incredibly beautiful that you couldn't really believe it.

There she stood in her beige, airy summer dress, her blonde hair falling openly over her back. After a while she slowly opened the buttons of her dress, one by one, and let it slide off her shoulders. I was delighted to learn that her dress was the only thing that covered her flawless body.

Now she looked into my eyes with a seductive smile and jumped headfirst into the water.

In no time I had also got rid of my clothes and jumped after her. We romped around the little kids and had fun. After a while we got out of the water, dried each other and surrendered to our lust.

First of all, the desire to eat.

It was only shortly after six in the evening, but the stomach of both of us hung close to the ground. And on this point the Corsican is like the normal French: baguette, salami, cheese and wine ... and everything is good. Only in this country everything tastes a little more powerful and spicy.

After that we sat for a while and talked about everything.

Then she suddenly stood up, shook my hand, pulled me out of the chair and walked slowly with me to the lawn, which, with a white sheet covered in partial shade, rocked back and forth in the warm breeze. Without saying anything, she directed me to the middle of the bed, half lay on top of me, and kissed me. And while she parted my lips very carefully with her tongue, she gripped my testicles with a hardly bearable tenderness and stroked them.

"I would like dessert now, you too?" she whispered to me between two kisses.

Sara is very slim with a flat stomach and small firm breasts, but when she hugs her body like this, it feels wonderfully soft and warm.

Yes, I really wanted an even bigger dessert.

I almost wanted to surrender to her and her hands at that moment, when I remembered that she did not yet know the real highlight of this bed construction.

"Dearest Sara, watch out now."

Then I make my arm very long and pull the split pin out of the lock. The frame and its contents slowly started to move.

Sara could hardly believe it, she crouched down, looked around and saw the bed moving towards the pool. When it got there, there was a little jerk and Sara fell on her back, now lying there with her arms outstretched and beaming at me.

Then she called in her well-known little schoolgirl manner:

"How cool is that, you just have to roll aside after fucking."

I hadn't thought that far at that moment.

Her eyes fixed on me, and suddenly she was transformed. Just the silly schoolgirl and now the pure seduction, which was absolutely aware of the effect of her dream body on me. We hadn't known each other that long, but I knew exactly how to interpret this slight flickering in her bright eyes:

I want you, I want to sleep with you. And now.

She was stretched out on her back, I crouched at her feet. Slowly she pulled her legs up, put her feet up and opened her legs in slow motion. I moved towards her on my knees and crouched very close between her widely spread thighs.

And then we played an incredibly awesome game with each other without any prior agreement, it just happened: Everything we did and said was only supposed to make the other person hot and ready to attack.

I looked at her gender, despite her legs wide open, the entrance to her vagina was completely covered by the outer labia and everything was still dry. I smiled at her and ran my hands gently along the inside of her thighs, far from her pubic.

"And you are sure that nobody can see us here?" She spoke very softly and slowly.

"Definitely ..."

"... and don't hear either?"

".. don't hear either ..."

"... not even if I scream loudly?"

"Here you can scream as loud as you want, except for me nobody will hear it."

I continued to slide my hands over her thighs, and the closer I got to her gender, the more blood flowed to the region and soon there was a tiny gap between her labia.

"What reason would you have to scream?" I winked at her.

"Don't know either ..."

With a little more pressure I ran my hands over the inside of her thighs and slid my thumbs over her perineum past her labia, without touching them directly. For the first time that evening, a soft, excited groan escaped from her open mouth and she lifted her butt very slightly towards my hands.

"Aha,

I repeated the procedure with the same result. The third time I let my thumbs slide very gently over her outer labia to get very close to the hidden clitoris at the top. With growing excitement, I noticed that the gap between her lips opened wider and it was already slightly glittering at the bottom. Her abdomen slowly but surely started to breathe and she breathed deeply.

When I saw her hands close around her breasts, I stepped in.

"Paws away."

I leaned over her, pushed her hands aside, and entered my mouth with my tongue.

"I'll do it myself." I whispered to her and, for a while, took turns sucking on her breasts.

"But you have to make a little effort ..."

In doing so, she pressed my head to her chest, I let my tongue circle over her small nipples, which she acknowledged with an audible groan.

After a while I straightened up and examined the results of my efforts between her legs. And they were clear.

Her lap had opened and her inner labia peeked out, shiny and damp, her little clitoris slowly ventured out of her hiding place, and a small trickle of her leaking body secretions seeped over her perineum.

With my thumbs I spread the smooth liquid on her pubic area and then gently and slowly massaged the entire region between her thighs with my flat hand. The longer I did that, the more movement came in her lap. She let her pelvis rotate, taking great care to put as little pressure on her gender as possible. Finally, I wanted to enjoy this intimate closeness to Sara for a while. The girl had her hands clawed sideways in the sheet, her whole body was now in motion and her lustful moaning was getting louder.

I leaned over her again, took her sweaty face in my hands soaked with her own juices and whispered to her:

"It almost sounds like my little Sara is really horny."

With one hand she pressed my head to her and shoved her tongue into my mouth, with the other she fished for my cock.

When she got hold of him, she grabbed it vigorously, jerked it, and then said in a breathless voice:

"And what should this little monster tell me ... which of us is probably hornier? Just watch your cock won't go back up until he's got me properly. "

And then she managed to grin cheekily at me despite her extreme excitement. That was mean and had to be avenged.

I loosened her hand from my penis and leaned over Sara so that he pressed lengthways against her vagina.

"Let that be my concern. You little beast will beseech me to finally push it in, rely on it."

Sara laughed at me.

"Come on, put it in me, fuck me, go ..."

She wriggled under me like an eel and tried to catch my cock.

I almost fell for it. And everything would have been perfectly prepared. My cock was rock hard, her lap open and wet.

"Come on, give me you little wild engraver."

Now, however, she had to laugh at herself at the stupidity. I knew then that she wasn't where I wanted her to be. That was provocation now. But I wanted her to die of lust and to lose all clear thinking from lust.

"Forget my darling ..."

I straightened up and looked at Sara's sweaty body. She looked into my eyes, breathing heavily, with anticipation, her upper body trembled in time with her breath, between her thighs the edges of her inner lips had already folded slightly outwards. The entrance my cock was supposed to enter was invitingly open and dripping with moisture.

Suddenly I leaned down to her and sank my mouth into her wide open lap. When I licked her clitoris, Sara screamed with delight and lust. A few times I let my tongue slide lengthwise between your labia up to her clitoris and thus increased her and my pleasure immeasurably. I let my tongue plunge into her wet vagina over and over again. It was pure pleasure to lick her inside of the wonderfully smooth, slippery skin and to taste her leaking juices. I felt the contractions of her lap, the trembling of her lower abdomen against my mouth, and I heard her loud moan of pleasure.

She really enjoyed what I was doing with her and I enjoyed doing it.

I straightened up one last time and looked at what I had done. There was a pleading bundle of lust, and I crouched in front of it with my mast erect. Sara's pelvis was spinning, her lap was urgently looking for something to rub against. I took my cock in my hand, bent it slightly down and said:

"Shut up."

She looked down at herself, completely distraught and impatient, and saw that my acorn was only a few inches from the entrance to her wet canal. I plowed my sex with my hard cock two or three times, then slowly pushed it through the slippery opening. The edges of her labia stretched around my bulging acorn until it was completely enclosed by them. Then I stopped my propulsion and pulled my tail back. Sara gasped with desire and desire. A few times I pushed the thickest part of my cock through the narrowest part of her boiling vagina and pulled myself out of it again, all in slow motion. With every penetration Sara bent and stretched her body towards me, moaning loudly.

For me, the resulting irritation was limited. But because I now also moved Sara's clitoris between my thumbs, it slowly but surely drove the girl crazy.

"Please go on ..." She literally screamed at me when I had just sunk my acorn into her again.

I stopped one last time, saw the girl lying in front of me, her long blonde hair stuck to her body, soaked in sweat, and breathing hard, she barely had control of her writhing slim body. The thick tip of my erection was in her expiring sex between her widely spread thighs.

Now she held out her arms to me and begged me:

"Please put it all in me, I can't stand it anymore, finally fuck me, biii ..."

She didn't get any further.

In a flowing movement, I pushed my erection all the way into her stomach and dropped onto her.

Sara acknowledged it with a long, redeeming "Jaaaaaaa ...."

I remained in this position for a few seconds, and then I did what she asked for.

I started to fuck Sara with slow, deep and powerful thrusts. And she raged under me. She screamed her lust uncontrollably, our sweaty bodies rubbed against each other, at the place of our union our bodies clapped on and into each other with an obscene-sounding smack. It was foreseeable that after this gigantic foreplay, the final act would be pretty short.

After just a few bumps, I felt the climax announcing itself in Sara, how her breath became even more hectic, how her hands clenched behind my back, how every muscle in her body tensed, the signs were clear.

And then Sara had an orgasm as you can wish for yourself and others: very violent and long lasting.

It started with staccato-like cries of pleasure, which slowly grew longer and more intense, and which then resulted in several slow waves of a hoarse and redeeming groan full of fervor and satisfaction.

And in one of these final waves I came with a force that clouded my senses.

As the fog slowly cleared, I felt that Sara's body was still twitching and throbbing, and I gave her time to regain my breath and consciousness.

I brushed the sweaty strands of hair from her face.

I had planned to give Sara the best possible satisfaction that evening. And when she fought me off completely, but laughed with bright and happy eyes, I knew that I didn't seem to have done too much wrong.

"Little Mattis down there probably hasn't noticed that the number is over."

Sara grinned at me. In fact, my erection was swollen significantly, but it was still enough to get stuck.

"He feels comfortable with you." I kissed her

"You are starting to get heavy for me."

"Oh, sorry .."

I was about to pull my cock out of her when something occurred to me:

"Say ... After fucking ... That's it now,

Sara immediately understood what I was getting at and looked aside.

"Do you think we can do it?"

"If you tried it, hold on."

I pressed my resection as deeply as possible into her lap, she clutched me tightly with my arms and legs, and then we gave the swing together. And after almost two rolls we fell into the refreshing water with a huge thump. In this constellation we sank almost to the bottom. Then she released her grip, I pulled my cock out of her warm cave and we drifted back to the surface separately.

We stayed in the water for a while and cooled our heated bodies, only to then warm them up and dry them again on the warm rock slab. The sun had disappeared behind the trees in the meantime, but it was still incredibly warm, and so it stayed the whole night, which still had a surprise to offer.

We ate and drank something else and discussed what will be thought of in the next few days. Sara's parents had been there last week. For her it was understandably a huge shock at first that her only daughter had thrown himself at the neck of some guy in Corsica. But we have come closer to each other, and apart from Sara being an adult, in the end they supported the decision and supported her daughter in everything that had to be settled.

Shortly after half past eleven and a bottle of red wine we decided to end the day. I pulled the bed back, we lay down under the sheet and let ourselves float back over the rump.

It was dark. We faced each other and kissed each other, actually, after this long and exhausting day, restful sleep was announced, but before that I had to confess something to Sara:

As a precaution , I had my hand this morning in view of what I had planned for the two of us placed. My premature ejaculation during our first sex had made me very unsettled. And when Sara was still sleeping next to me this morning, I had hand-made my morning batten to relieve the pressure.

"What, you got one down right next to me?"

Sara's voice sounded like a mixture of horror and surprise.

"Oh Sara, I only did that because I was scared of hosing off too early. I also had a hard on, and you were lying asleep next to me, your shirt had slipped and your sweet breasts were exposed washed up, it was pretty quick. "

Sara said nothing more, but I felt her eyes on me. Because of the darkness, I could barely make out her pretty face. If it had been light, the telltale flicker would have been in her eyes again. But so at first I was immeasurably unsettled and then completely surprised when she suddenly pushed her naked body against me very slowly and whispered in my ear hardly audibly:

"Then you bastard had a climax more than I did today,

Then this little beast bit me in the earlobe and added:

"... but I'll get it from you now."

It spoke and disappeared under the sheet. She kissed slowly over my chest. I held my breath. We'd screwed our brains a few hours ago, but Sara still didn't have enough.

She had never put my cock in her mouth before. A few days ago, she had spoiled him with a multitude of small kisses, which drove me crazy. But she didn't have it in her mouth yet, and I didn't want to push her to do it. And now suddenly she sucked in my little wobble completely without warning and worked it on with my tongue and palate, so that the sweat broke out suddenly. Now it was me who groaned and clasped his hands in the sheet.

The poor girl, however, had to struggle for a few minutes until my erection reached a consistency that approximated the upcoming requirements. Then she left the rest to the strength of her vaginal muscles.

She leaned over me, straightened my cock, inserted it, and sank down on it. Her interior was adequately lubricated by our shared body fluids, and she could start her ride on me unhindered.

I lay there and was completely fascinated by what was happening to me. In the dark I could only vaguely see Sara's slim body moving on my lap. Her head was bent back, her hair stroked my legs in time with her rhythm. Their ride was strangely silent, only a very light, barely audible wet smack from the place of our association was heard.

An incredible feeling of happiness flowed through me. A few weeks

ago I was the personified sexual emergency area, and now that. It's not just the great sex I'm allowed to have with Sara, she's an extraordinary person in many ways. On the one hand so spontaneously that she turns her entire life upside down and simply stays with me here on the island following love, but on the other hand with very clear ideas of how she continues to pursue and develop her original plans with great self-confidence

.

After graduation, she actually wanted to study political science and journalism. And in the first week of our life together, she was already looking for the possibility of distance learning. For example, this was something that I had completely neglected so far, since I had initially restricted myself to my manual skills.

I am fascinated by intelligent women who know what they want and take what they need.

And in those minutes she wanted me. She wanted another orgasm. She also knew how to help her except that my stiff penis was in her. And she claimed it.

I was so caught up in my thoughts and so impressed with what I saw and felt that I completely forgave Sara's needs. After a few minutes, she took my hands that I had placed on her thighs and led them to her breasts. The tips of her breasts were erect and firm, and when I rubbed them between my fingers, Sara immediately accelerated the pace of her ride on me, and for the first time a clear gasp escaped her open mouth. She also started to move her lap with a routing movement on my cock, which was deep inside her.

The girl's condition was remarkable, she had had a hard day, then our sweaty, uninhibited sex a few hours ago and now this long ride ...

I straightened up and put my lips over her left breast, gently sucked it in and licked over her hard nipple.

As a result of this treatment, Sara started slowly but surely. She pressed my head to her chest that I had trouble loosening myself to give the treatment to the right side. The final finale came when, sitting across from me, crossed her legs behind my back and pressed her body against me and my stiff cock with all my strength.

I love this position because I feel like I am savoring her hot channel to the bottom.

Sara came in several bursts accompanied by a loud, relieving groan. Once again I held her in my arms and waited for the pulsing throbbing inside her lap to subside.

This deep massage of my member was responsible for the fact that I was one orgasm ahead of her at the end of the day, because I was caught again in that second.

Sara shouldn't have registered it because the girl was now hanging in my arms. I couldn't help but smile, because I actually managed to get my beloved Sara into a coma.

I gently let her slide from my lap next to me onto the bed and covered her. I stroked her hair from her face and gave her a kiss.

She was asleep two minutes later.

And I lie there, looking up at the starry sky, which is splendidly spreading out in front of me, and I suddenly realize that I am probably the happiest person in the world.

So happy that I wonder if I shouldn't have a guilty conscience.

No I do not have to!

The End.

The experiment

Jana looked at the camera. The lens was on the couch where she and her best friend Fiona had sat. The two 20-year-olds looked at each other indecisively and then looked around the room. They were among themselves. The camera on a tripod was a good two meters away from them and would record their every move. The window curtains were drawn. The ceiling lamp gave off dull light. The couch had a black leather cover and felt cold under her butt. Jana's bare legs stuck to the material. She was nervous, sweating and wondering again what she was doing here. She gave Fiona a questioning look. "Are you ready?"

"No ... you?"

A shake of her friend's head confirmed that it wasn't. Jana sighed and shrugged. "It doesn't help. We have to go through that now. Do we want to? "

Three days earlier:

" You could do me a huge favor if you take part. "

Jana and Fiona looked at Lisa in disbelief. The psychology student had just made a request to the friends that had sounded so incredible that the two of them didn't know what they were up to. Jana frowned, Fiona raised an eyebrow.

"And what exactly should we do?" Asked Jana.

Lisa took a deep breath and gathered. Then she looked deep into the eyes of the other two and specified her request. "I already said that you should take part in a sexual experiment."

"Yes, we understood that," said Fiona. "Just not why, and what exactly you expect from us."

"Then let me explain it to you," Lisa suggested, suddenly looking determined. "I have to submit my seminar paper, and I have chosen a topic that is not everyday and that will certainly cause excitement."

Jana was silent while Fiona smiled. Lisa was not impressed and continued her explanation. "I chose the subject of masturbation. However, I will not talk about simple masturbation, but I will deal with a much more interesting approach. "

" To what extent? "Jana asked.

"Where and when do we usually satisfy ourselves?"

"What ... you satisfy yourself? What kind of depraved are you!", Fiona Lisa teased, grinning up to both ears. Jana also enjoyed the joke at Lisa's expense.

Lisa went over the top and said: "Masturbation is always a very private moment, where we are for ourselves and where we concentrate on our needs. Nobody is watching us, nobody is taking part in our private experience. "

" Would be even nicer if we had an audience, "Jana said with a cheeky grin.

"But that's exactly the point," said Lisa. "What would change for you if you had spectators?"

"Huh?"

"Have you ever been caught masturbating by your parents?"

Jana winced. "I prefer not to answer the question."

Lisa and Fiona grinned. Even if Jana hadn't given an answer, it was obvious. Lisa turned to Jana and said: "And if you get caught, you usually stop what you're busy because it's a very private moment and you don't want to share it with anyone."

Fiona nodded in agreement.

"Jana .. Have you ever masturbated with a friend? "

Jana looked at Lisa in confusion. "No ... Of course not."

"Why not?"

Jana looked at Lisa in astonishment. "It sounds like it is normal to meet and play around with others."

"No, it's not that," Lisa said. "But apparently you had a good reason not to trust a friend and do it with her."

"Have you already?" Fiona wanted to know from Lisa.

"This is not about me," Lisa evaded, whereupon Fiona grinned with satisfaction.

Lisa ignored her friend's reaction and continued. "My work is about how people react when they don't have the usual privacy during

masturbation ." "I don't get it," Jana admitted. "What are you trying to prove?"

Lisa sighed and thought for a moment. "I would like to ask you both to be available for my experiment. I want you to masturbate together.

"What?"

"Do you still have them all?"

"You are crazy."

"Never in life."

Lisa let her friends express her displeasure and continued her explanation after Jana and Fiona calmed down a bit. "I expected this reaction. Well ... have you two ever satisfied yourself in front of each other? "

" Of course not, "replied Fiona firmly.

"And I don't intend to," added Jana.

Lisa nodded. "I am interested in the question of whether you can find peace and let yourself go, even if you are not alone. If you are not alone in bed or in the The tub is lying and someone is sitting next to you, who is watching you, gets close to your feelings and does the same as you do. "

"That will never be allowed as a seminar paper," Jana was sure.

"We'll see," avoided Lisa. "The question is whether you would be able to open up to your best friend and stroke you in her presence. I would then like to measure your pulse using a heart rate monitor and read how excited you are. "

" Sounds totally stupid, "said Jana. Fiona said nothing.

"The whole thing would be a kind of stressful situation for you."

"And why don't you do it yourself?" Asked Jana curiously.

"I have to watch the experiment and draw my conclusions from it. I can't see the experiment as a neutral and distant participant, "Lisa explained to her.

Her friends were pouting and irritated in front of her. "Come on ... you'd do me a big favor."

"Why don't you ask people on the street and offer them a small allowance?" Asked Fiona. "Surely there are some crazy people who would do that."

"For one thing, I don't have the time, I have to give up work at the end of the week."

"What?" It blurted out of Jana. "How did you waste the time?"

"I was concentrating on a different topic at first, but it was far too boring," said Lisa desperately. "I want to do a really good job that will attract attention. Please ... Can't you help me?"

Jana and Fiona looked at each other questioningly.

Fiona shrugged. "Actually, I never wished to see you playing around with your pussy."

"Who says I'm satisfied?" Joked Jana.

"Please ... I don't know what else to do," Lisa emphasized the urgency of the matter.

"But Fiona and I would remain anonymous?"

"Naturally. Your names don't appear anywhere. "

" And would you watch us? "Jana wanted to know.

"I would be in a different room. You would be among you and undisturbed. "

" And then how exactly do you want to draw your insights from the matter when you are not there? "Fiona was irritated.

Lisa pressed around and struggled for words. Then she took turns looking at her friends and said, "Did I mention that a camera on a tripod will be pointed at you all the time?"

"Huh?"

"What?"

Jana and Fiona protested again and didn't want to believe what Lisa suggested to them. Lisa waited a moment and then started to explain. "The camera is part of the experiment. Just as you have to deal with that Sitting next to you doing the same thing, the camera is also a challenge. It should show whether, despite the camera, you are able to concentrate and enjoy your task. "

"And are you taking us in or what?"

"I'm going to sit in another room and watch you on a screen," Lisa admitted.

"Do you want to get mad on us or what?" Asked Jana with a grin.

"I don't mean to," Lisa said. "It's all about my project."

"Will there be a recording?" Fiona asked.

"There will be a recording, but I won't show it to anyone."

"Then why do you need it?" Asked Jana curiously.

"Because I might have to watch the scene several times to consolidate my impressions."

"Or to get you started," Jana repeated her guess.

Lisa ignored the charge and continued to explain her motives. "Maybe I have to prove that I didn't suck it all out of my fingers."

"So you're going to make the picture of us public?" Asked Fiona with a skeptical tone in her voice.

"I'm not going to release the whole film. I may have to present parts of the recording, but then you won't be recognizable, "Lisa promised.

" Are you going to put black bars in front of us or what? "

"Something like that. But first of all I have no intention of showing the video to anyone. Unless you want a copy. "

" We didn't agree, "said Jana.

"I'm asking you ... I don't know how to quickly find other participants. And I can't steal anything new at short notice either. Come on. "

Today

Jana and Fiona were sitting on the couch in the living room of Lisa's apartment. Lisa was in her bedroom and would watch the events in the living room via her laptop. Jana and Fiona were sitting as ordered and not picked up in their seats and still couldn't believe they'd gotten involved in this madness. Jana stared incredulously at a side table next to the couch where Lisa had placed a box, which the friends should open as soon as the experiment started.

"I'm ready. You can get started! "Lisa called from the living room door.

Jana hesitated briefly and then took off the lid of the box. She discovered various sex toys that were confused in the box. Jana recognized two vibrators, a dildo and lubricating cream. She also identified love pearls and a lay-on vibrator.

"Lisa seems to be well equipped," she said to Fiona.

Fiona looked at the selection of utensils and asked: "Are they your own? Should we use them, even though they knew who they were in?"

"We don't have to use those things."

Jana eyed the camera. She realized that Lisa would follow her every move on the laptop. She giggled and turned to Fiona. "Not only that you are sitting next to me Spy in the bedroom will be able to watch everything closely.

"Is the sound actually being recorded?"

"Certainly. So moan loudly," joked Jana. "Shall we?"

The friends had long and broadly discussed the upcoming challenge. They had weighed up the pros and cons and had agreed to help their friend Lisa. At least they wanted to try to get involved in the experiment It remained to be seen, both sexually experienced and satisfied for many years, but none of them had ever tried anything comparable before Jana glanced at her heart rate monitor, which would also provide information about her state of mind to Lisa.

Jana touched the button placket of her blouse. In addition she wore a short cloth skirt, the hem of which reached half of her thighs. Fiona watched her curiously, but held back.

"And you?"

Jana gave her an encouraging look, whereupon Fiona gave a jerk and took off her top. A black bra emerged that housed a handsome breast. In contrast to Jana, Fiona was not slim and showed slight love handles at one point or another. The waist was not so slim, the butt bulging, and the legs thicker than those of her friend. But the blonde with shoulder-length hair had a pretty face and could not complain about a lack of interest in her person from the direction of the men's world. Jana, with the short dark hair, was slim as a crop and had a rather modest stem, which, however, matched her stature well.

Jana opened her blouse, revealing her bare skin. She hardly ever wore a bra. Fiona and she had agreed with Lisa that the camera would keep an eye on them at all times and that they shouldn't try to hide their nakedness. You should act as relaxed and relaxed as if you were alone. That meant, of course, that they would reveal their breasts and the area between their thighs, but that would certainly not be a problem, Lisa thought. At least this was not a challenge between the friends, since Jana and Fiona had met naked several times. However, never for the purpose of mutual masturbation, but rather in the locker room at home.

Fiona rose from her seat and brushed down her pants. Dressed only in bra and matching panties, she sat down again and waited until her friend had taken off more clothing. Jana decided to take off her shorts as well and stayed next to Fiona with white panties and an open blouse.

"And now?"

"Now you have to get horny," Fiona joked, grinning mischievously.

"Should I just start now?"

Fiona shrugged. "The beginning is probably the hardest. Please hand over one of the vibrators."

Jana reached into the box and found a silver vibrator, which she handed over to Fiona. She herself decided on the lay-on vibrator, which she eyed curiously. "I've never encountered anything like this."

"I was ... such a person is very nice," Fiona knew. She turned on the vibrator, which was in a classic form, and watched the buzzing wand in her hand. Jana struggled to turn on her device. When she did, she held the bottom of the device to her thigh and let the vibration work.

Fiona watched her and in turn put the pleasure stick on her leg.

"But you already know that the vibrator has to go somewhere else, don't you?" Joked Jana.

"Can you imagine Lisa using all of the equipment herself?"

"Hopefully she cleaned it up properly," replied Jana, grinning.

The friends pushed their toys over their thighs but didn't dare to take them to where they should normally be used.

"Do you currently have such a hang-up thing?" Asked Jana curiously.

Fiona shook her head. "Not currently. My device has given up at some point."

"

Overused ?" Fiona grinned. "Not that. And I tried it with new batteries too. Seems to have been a piece of Monday equipment."

"Is there no longer a guarantee?" Jana asked.

"Would you complain about a vibrator,

Jana thought about it. "Probably not. Could lead to embarrassing glances from the salesperson. "

" The best thing to do is to order online because everything is a little more discreet, "Fiona suggested.

"How many different sex toys do you have?" Asked Jana curiously, who was playing for time and was not yet ready to

heat up . Fiona let her buzzing pleasure stick slide over both legs, stomach and over the bra and thought. " Actually only a vibrator that can be set to five levels and a dildo that I hardly ever use. "

"Then why do you have it?"

"I wanted to have a part that I can use in the bath," Fiona admitted in a low voice.

"And?"

"Nothing and ...

Jana rolled her eyes. She looked at her vibrator, which she was now gently moving around her belly button, and asked. "So you got it in the bathtub with that thing."

"Yeah, right."

"Was it nice?"

"Mm."

Jana realized that she could not get out of Fiona for the moment and decided to look into the borrowed giver of joy. The lay-on vibrator could be set to different levels and she tried each one. Curiously she pushed the device under the blouse and shortly afterwards felt the comforting tingling of the vibrator on her nipple. "Not bad."

Fiona looked over at her. She herself had carried her copy between her legs and rubbed it gently over the inside of the thigh. None of the friends yet dared to approach their intimate areas. Jana suddenly laughed.

"What is it?"

"I'm trying to imagine yourself lying in the bathtub and pushing in a rubber bump."

Fiona joined the laugh. Jana reached into the box and pulled out a skin-colored artificial penis, which was a good 20 centimeters in length. "How about this?"

"Maybe later," Fiona said gently and fixed the camera. "Don't you get nervous about being filmed?"

"Yes," Jana confirmed. "I'm trying to hide it as much as possible. I just have to remember that afterward strangers look at how I got it."

"Thank you Jana, now I'm imagining exactly that."

Jana grinned and decided to enjoy the vibration of her joy donor where the main area of ??application of the device was. She kept her panties on and spread her legs. Pushed down from the breasts she laid the vibrator down her belly and passed the waistband of her panties. She had chosen a medium vibration level and carefully pushed the part at the level of her labia. She cocked her head and concentrated on the feeling between her legs. When she grinned suddenly asked Fiona: "And?"

"It's all right." "

Now Fiona followed her friend's example and laid the vibrator lengthwise on her pussy. The layer of fabric on the panties prevented direct contact with the device, and yet the vibrating thing was quite irritating." Hui. .. Not bad."

"You probably won't be horny."

"Nonsense, not me."

The friends looked at each other and grinned at each other. Then they glanced between the legs of each other and watched curiously as the toys buzzed happily in front of them. After a while Jana pulled her hand back and switched off the device.

"Have you had enough?" Asked Fiona in astonishment.

"No. I just wanted to look at something else."

She reached into the box and got hold of the love balls. She slid the plastic balls between her fingers and eyed them curiously.

"Do you want to try them out now?" Asked Fiona.

"Why not? I've never used things like that before. You?"

"Not yet," Fiona admitted.

Jana held the end of the string between her thumb and forefinger and inspected the balls that were attached a few centimeters apart. "What if the string breaks and things get stuck?"

"Then Lisa will drive you to the hospital afterwards," joked Fiona and looked expectantly at Jana.

When Jana did not take action even after half a minute, Fiona asked. "Don't you dare?"

"Yes ... Only I'll have to take my panties off for this ... I'll do it if you have fun with Lisa's dildo at the same time."

Fiona raised her eyebrows. "Do you really want to watch how I get it?"

"Sure. It sure looks sharp."

With a mischievous smile on her lips, Jana briefly raised her butt and pulled down her panties. She kept her blouse on. She rummaged in the box and took out the tube with the lubricant. She took a strand of the lotion and spread it between her labia. Fiona watched intently and made no move to follow her friend's example. Jana wiped her slippery fingers on her blouse and looked at her shiny pussy. "It should be properly lubricated now."

Fiona grinned and looked between her companion's legs. Jana's abdomen was hairless. She had a small dolphin tattoo above her column. The beak-like mouth of the animal pointed towards Jana's pussy. Jana examined the love balls with a critical eye and led the bottom ball on the string to her column. She pushed the ball in and held her breath. When the first bullet was in her pussy, she tackled the second.

"Hopefully everyone will fit in at all," she joked. Fiona was still staring fascinated at her friend's lap. Jana noticed her interest and asked: "What about you?"

"Then give me the dildo and the lubricating cream."

Jana reached into the box with her free hand and handed over the artificial tail and then the cream. Fiona took both and put the things next to her on the couch. Then she grabbed her panties and pulled it down. Jana watched curiously and looked at Fiona's lap with interest, where light pubic hair grew discreetly over her friend's column. Fiona dripped a blob of the lube on the dildo and spread it on the top of the toy. Then Fiona put the wand between her legs, grinned at the camera, and pushed the first few inches of the dildo into her pussy.

Jana grinned as she watched her friend's reaction. Fiona held her breath, rolled her eyes and made a hilarious grimace as the art phallus pierced Fiona's pussy inch by inch.

Jana found the sight special, but not even uninteresting. "Looks kind of sharp."

"You're not going to get horny from watching now, are you?" Asked Fiona, pausing in her movement and refusing to take up the baton.

Jana shrugged and grinned. "I should be lying if I said that what you're doing doesn't matter to me a little."

"What about you? Where's the second ball?"

Jana reflected on her lap and started the next bullet. Out of the corner of her eye, she saw Fiona gently move the pleasure stick back and forth in her pussy. After two thirds of the toy was on the belt, she looked at the last ball with a skeptical eye. "Is the third one still going?"

"Try it out," recommended Fiona, who was constantly fucking her artificial penis.

Jana's breath caught as the third bullet set off to disappear between her labia too. "When I think that they were in Lisa before ..."

Fiona looked curiously at Jana's lap, but didn't interrupt her gentle movements. "And?"

"I probably couldn't run anymore. And now?"

"Pull the cord."

Jana picked up the suggestion and pulled the cord that protruded between the labia. Before she knew it, the last bullet jumped out.

"You must have pulled too tight," said Fiona, grinning .

Jana pushed the ball back in and tugged less on the cord. She felt the balls move slightly inside. "But I don't find it really tingly ... And with you?

"

Jana freed herself from the love balls and thoughtfully stroked her pussy. The labia were smeared thanks to the lubricating cream. She watched Fiona for a while as she had fun with Lisa's dildo, then snatched the vibrator out of the box and put it into operation. She chose the middle level and slowly pushed the wand into her pussy. "Oh, not bad."

"Do you actually prefer to use your vibrators outside or do you prefer to push them in like you do now?" Asked Fiona curiously, who now seemed much more relaxed than just a few minutes ago.

Jana shrugged. "Sometimes like this; sometimes like that. It feels awesome when everything vibrates in me ... But often it's enough for me to apply the part externally. "

Fiona looked at the camera and nodded at it. "Do you think Lisa is now sitting in front of the laptop and is getting horny?"

"Definitely," Jana was sure. "Maybe she also kept some sex staff for herself that she is now using."

Fiona liked the idea and grinned mischievously. "Do you actually know that we could sell this well as porn?"

"Right. Maybe we should turn this into money here. "

" Then let's shoot some sharp video clips of ourselves in the near future, in which we spoil ourselves with different toys, "Fiona suggested with a broad grin.

Jana was amused, but the next moment she was confronted with a tip of pleasure that the vibrating wand had triggered in her pussy.

"Does it work?" Asked Fiona curiously.

"Not with you?" Asked Jana back in a husky voice.

Fiona grinned. "I don't want to anticipate the evaluation of the experiment, but the way it looks, it turns out to be a complete success."

Jana nodded in agreement and increased the vibration by one step. She looked over at Fiona, who was moving at a much faster pace Tag put on as before. "Are you getting horny?"

Fiona closed her eyes and nodded silently. With both hands she pushed the dildo into the pussy and sighed again and again. Jana found that she no longer had to hold back and let out a loud cry of joy. She pampered herself with the vibrator for a while and then pulled it back. She slipped her finger into her pussy and noticed how wet she was. Suddenly an idea came to her.

"Will you lend me your dildo?"

"It belongs to Lisa ... but gladly."

She pulled the fake tail out of her pussy with a smacking sound and held it out to Jana.

"It's completely glued," Jana grinned and took the stick. Without hesitation, she put the dildo that had been in her friend until just between her legs and pushed the good piece inch by inch into herself.

Fiona watched the whole thing curiously and played with her fingers on her column. Jana looked at her lap and said: "Do you need a new toy?"

"My fingers are enough for now."

While Jana was enjoying the hostess' dildo, Fiona's fingers quickly slid over her clit. Both women groaned and made no secret of their great lust. For a brief moment Jana wondered if she should approach Fiona. Since she could not estimate whether Fiona would be ready for this, she refrained from the idea. At least as part of this experiment.

"You know," Jana explained in a husky voice. "It's not that bad to masturbate with a friend."

Fiona passionately fingered the pussy and nodded silently. Then she let out a sigh that had washed. Jana became aware of the reaction and looked at her friend curiously. Fiona jumped violently at that moment. Her finger raced at high speed over her clit. She groaned and screamed, rolled her eyes, threw her head back and could not and did not want to hide the fact that she was being struck by a gigantic orgasm.

Jana was so impressed by the sight that she rammed the dildo between her legs more powerfully and became hotter with every push. Fiona had left the peak of her climax behind and was enjoying the fading fades of her pleasure. She only noticed marginally how Jana turned onto the road of redemption and brought herself to a fulminant orgasm with a sharp cry.

"Oooooaaaah ... I'm coming!"

Her body jerked to herself as the waves of pleasure whipped through her body. She squirmed on the couch and moaned her joy beyond enjoying the world. After a while the cool feeling subsided and gave way to broad satisfaction. When Jana opened her eyes and looked aside, she saw Fiona grinning broadly. The friends looked at each other and smiled at each other.

"Who would have thought it could be such an awesome experience?" Jana stated.

"It definitely exceeded my expectations."

"Is Lisa happy with the experiment?"

As if on command, the living room door opened and Lisa entered the room. She grinned cheekily and went to the couch. She put her hands on her hips and shook her head. "Do you actually know what number you just pulled off ... insanity."

"Hopefully it will help you with your project," said Fiona, smiling broadly.

Jana frowned. "Tell me, Lisa ... why are the buttons of your blouse buttoned offset?"

Fiona looked and Lisa also checked the button panel.

"Exactly ... And the zipper on your pants is open," said Fiona firmly. "You didn't ... While we were experimenting here ... Did you?"

Jana jumped on the train. "Now don't say that you got horny with us and got yourself in front of your laptop ... You were actually going to monitor the experiment."

Lisa looked down and grinned sheepishly. Then she shrugged, saw her friends apologetically and said: "What should I talk about ...? How you made yourself hot was just so cool ... I just had to stroke myself."

"Why didn't you join us?" Jana asked.

"I thought about it first, but I didn't want to endanger the experiment," said Lisa.

"It's a shame," said Jana. "Mm."

"What?"

> "Now that the experiment is over ... what do you think if you keep us company and the three of us lose ourselves with your toys?"

The End.

Don't you wanna cheat me

What would you say if your wife told you without any warning that she would like to see you fuck another woman? In any case, I was completely horrified! Can this be? My dear wife asks me to have an affair? What may sound like a dream to some must have some reason!

I became suspicious. Did she have a lover herself? As long as we're together, I've never cheated on her, either before or after the wedding. I would not have even considered an affair in a dream, I was happy - even with our love life.

After I got myself together again, I clearly told her what I thought of her proposal. But with her magical smile, at least she made me think about it - in theory. But at least in my subconscious it has been working ever since.

And the more I remembered our conversation, the more I had to admit how excited the thought was.

Finally, I imagined more and more what it would be like at my age with an exciting young woman, without a guilty conscience towards my wife, yes I would even do her a favor.

For a long time I hadn't gotten so horny so often since I had these thoughts regularly. To do this, you need to know the following: My wife is not particularly visually attractive.

Nevertheless, I adore her and, as I said, I am completely satisfied with our love life. Still, I never stopped looking at pretty young women, on the street, in shops, in everyday life.

In short, six days after her suggestion, I asked her carefully how serious she was. She just smiled at me and said: "This new swingers club just opened in the neighboring town!"

"Oh and there should I go with YOU?"

"Nn-no, go alone for the first time and tell me everything. Maybe you'll take me a second time ...? "

Said and done.

Three days later I was able to tell my loved ones about my experiences.

It started a bit hesitant and unusual for me. At the beginning I stood in front of a French wall and looked at several couples blowing, licking and birding. Some of the ladies present seemed to be taken with me. Little by little I felt gentle hands on my buttocks, legs or even on my chest. I liked these touches, but I still felt a bit strange and, yes, inhibited.

But then I discovered an unoccupied hot tub for up to eight people. I got in, naked. In the pool, my erection was not visible to everyone, which was fine with me as a newcomer.

Suddenly an about thirty-year-old brunette, whom I had noticed before, appeared and took a seat right next to me. After a little small talk I got braver, took her hand and put it on my leg. I soon felt her fingers on my cock.

Tanja, as her name is, soon blew my bulky pole under water and only showed up grinning from time to time to take a breath. A real horny bitch, she was really good at it, not as awkward as my own wife ...

It didn't take long and a second swinger bent over me so that my tongue could reach her teasing breasts, her belly and then her crotch .

Of course I also licked her column extensively while Tanja blew my cock unchanged. I licked the hot crack several times in a row. The bitch trembled and trembled with each stroke of the tongue.

Finally she grabbed the back of my head and forcibly pressed it onto her dripping cunt. As I fucked her with my tongue, I gasped for breath.

I groaned in her cunt, but I almost couldn't breathe because her twitching abdomen almost completely closed my mouth and nostrils. At the same time I felt Tanja try to detach myself from my cock to show up and gasp for breath, but automatically I grabbed her head and pressed it back onto my cock under water.

I thought my whole body was on fire, felt my blood running through my veins. Tanja's tongue made my cock explode in her mouth, my hands fell off her head and she took a deep breath out of the water.

But I was still caught and licked the strange overflowing cunt as if it were about my life. And it actually worked that way ...

The bitch gasped above me and I felt her body tense as my tongue kept thrusting between her pussy lips and deep into her grotto.

I stuck my tongue between her wet, shimmering lips. I flicked her crevice before entering her cave again. I had now learned to deal with my shortness of breath. The taste of this woman was just fantastic, no comparison with my wife at home. My tail, which had just been juiced, straightened up again under water, while the foreign cunt juices ran over my chin into the water.

The lady on my face trembled under a powerful orgasm, her body reared and splashed into the pool in front of me. I took a deep breath.

I don't remember ever being as pointed before as now, neither with my wife nor before our marriage. My pleasure stick was again vertical under water like a one.

The stranger had left, but Tanja was still standing a few meters from the pool and continued to watch us. She was naked except for a white panties and - started to pee! A dark spot grew in the middle of her panties before her golden sparkling wine ran out of the fabric. I had never seen it like this! Tanja now walked up to me and just let it go. When she stood in front of me at the poolside and looked down at me, her streaked legs shimmered in the light of the indirect lighting.

Tanja now sat next to me on the edge of the pool, I turned to her and stood in front of her between her open thighs. I felt the pungent urine smell, which surprisingly did not repel me, but even exfoliated. "Lick me ..." Tanja breathed towards me in a trembling voice. My head was already flying on autopilot. I obeyed. At first I gently approached the dark spot on Tanja's panties with the tip of my tongue, which was still getting bigger. Finally I was in the target area. My tongue curiously ran over the wet fabric. It was now soaking wet, especially since Tanja kept on whirling. The taste wasn't too bad. I expected something terrible, but it was half as wild. Somehow it was really cool and I couldn't get enough. Tanja put up with my treatment for quite a while until the tip of my tongue obviously hit a critical point. Tanja's body tightened and she groaned.

> Not long after, I was standing in front of my own front door again and fiddled with the front door bowl from my pocket. How would my darling react if I told her everything?

The End.

Never laugh at witches

Never

laugh at witches' stupid titles. I know. But once you've read that, you might disagree. A young girl told me all of this. Around 14, 15. At first I wanted to laugh. But then she told me about my most secret secrets. Those from school. The only three people knew. One was me, the other was my Klaudia, and the third was my best friend.

Warning!!!

If you don't believe in witches, keep your opinion to yourself. Hide them inside of you. For heaven's sake never say it openly or loudly. Because they can hear you!

What is?

You think I'm stupid?

You motherfucker don't know what's going on.

The thing is that I didn't believe in them. Wished they existed, yes I did.

I read "Lord of the Rings" 3 or 4 times. I have it as an audio book. I have the Extendend version at home. I saw it 10 times or more. I could even memorize passages of the text.

Loved DSA and Baldurs Gate.

Listened inspired by King Arthur and Merlin. From Morgana and Avalon, from the stone circles.

I really wanted to go into this time.

I would see Elves how Sam exclaimed in "Lord of the Rings" when Aragon told him that she was going to Rivendell would go to Elron's house. Unicorns, gnomes, elves, wizards and witches.

That was what I longed for. The realm of mythology, fables and imagination.

But as I said:

WAS!

1 The history

But the best thing to do is to start with the beginning. Don't be surprised at the spelling. But I have to tell you that I was a man in the best (?) Years not quite three months ago.

54 years, reasonably healthy, except for a few age-related ailments.

I took everything I could get in my life.

I had my first fuck when I was 22, but from there it went uphill.

My youngest was 12, so I don't want to show off. She looked really cool. Giant boobs, great figure, an abortion behind. You don't expect that she is only 12.

My oldest was 45. And that was when I was under 30.

Anyway, I thought she was my oldest.

But more on that later.

Faithful at first, this virtue wore off over the years.

But this also subsided with age. I was glad when I got one in front of the pipe.

It all changed suddenly when I met Roxana.

It was a really cool device. Huge plump tits, narrow waist, so really great figure, bubble butt, long legs, long hair, cute face. So what you have as an indication, always in bed or want to have fucked.

But she really looked that way. Although "ER" was no longer so good, or my head hung too quickly, I made myself a "penis ring", it has not been able to stop since she was with me. Worse than when I was young, where I sometimes wanked up to 5 times a day. But with her I burst into unprecedented heights.

I often told her that she must have enchanted me. I haven't been so horny in years, not so potent in decades.

And she replied to me that she was a witch.

Of course I laughed at her. But then she always looked at me angrily. So over time I didn't. I just nodded and thought my part.

2 The fateful look

Then that fateful day came.

I went shopping with Roxana. We had bought several hot articles to cover her hot body. You know. Bra, panties, nightwear, a new horny corset.

She wore what every man liked to see.

Another prejudice.

Hardly any woman wears a corset at work during the day. Especially not with suspenders and without panties. But I could come home whenever I wanted, she was always wearing exactly what I had introduced to her when I was out and about. And before my jacket fell to the floor, she had my spanking in one of her three openings. It was just great. I always got exactly what I wanted.

But then it happened.

As I said, we were expanding your laundry inventory every month. A very young girl came towards us. About 12, 13 years old.

In contrast to my youth, at that time the girls only started getting breasts at the age of 13 or 14, with a few exceptions, they are already carriers of "C" when they are 12. Maybe "B".

And this girl had to wear at least "C". If not more. I quickly appraised her. Tight sweater, wide mini skirt, tights, shoes with heels, long legs, great figure, big boobs that didn't seem to hang, brown eyes (Brown eyes, coffee crap - make all men jeck), nice smile, white teeth, red curly mane with bangs .. When I turned to her I saw that her hair went to her bottom and fell so wide that from her body to there was nothing to see her bottom, and then there was a gust of wind. He blew her skirt up and showed me a thong under her tights that left both buttocks free.

My spanking immediately stood. "I want to fuck her, now, immediately until that I'm falling dead, "I thought to myself.

Then I felt a knock in my ribs. I turned to Roxana, startled.

"You will pay for me," she said with evil, sparkling eyes.

Nothing more. Only: "You will pay for me".

It stayed in my arm, but said nothing all day.

Neither do I. I was guilty. She had seen my look, which only said: "I want to fuck you". But I didn't mean her.

The night was calm. She left me alone and I didn't dare touch her, let alone apologize to her. The next day I came home from work. I saw this girl again just outside the front door. Today she was wearing a blue wide mini dress, in which the skirt part never deserved to be called "skirt". My pants almost burst with lust. And when she passed me, she smiled at me. If we had been on a desert island, me would have raped her now. Several times. And in all three holes.

She was pure sex par excellence. The perfect sperm robber. The only real fuck bitch. And I suddenly didn't give a shit how old she was. Something I used to do loathed, I somehow freaked out with her.

When I got into the apartment, the freezing cold hit me. Roxana stood in the hallway with her arms crossed. I closed the door and went up to her. Her hand shot forward with lightning speed. I stopped as if paralyzed. The second hand jerked forward. And I could have sworn a blue lightning bolt shot out of her, straight at me. I don't know anything else.

3 Excuse me

In the morning I found myself in our pajamas in our bed. Roxana made breakfast. Had I dreamed of lightning? But if not, what had I done last night?

When I drove to work, I was still pondering the lost evening. At the railroad barrier I waited for the train to come and for it to go up again. Then there was a knock on my passenger window. My breath caught. That was it! Today a white blouse under which you could see that she wasn't wearing a bra. The areola looked dark, the warts almost stuck through the thin synthetic blouse.

I let the window down and she leaned into the car, her tits almost falling out. In any case, I could look very far into her blouse. Needless to say, my cock in the pants was fighting the zipper. And what it looked like this time my cock would win. The seams were already groaning.

"Excuse me, can you help me? I got lost. "

"Where do you want to go?"

"To Hohenstaufen Castle."

Well, it was more of a ruin. I knew her. Behind the rail barrier on the left, then 15 km through the mountains, then you stood in front of her. But I didn't tell her that.

“But there is still a long way to go. You will have to walk there for at least three hours. "

Her smile died.

" So far? "

"Yes. But if you want, I can take you with me, I have to go there too. "

And then I'll fuck you. There is no pig at this time of year. And nobody will hear you scream.

I didn't care anything. Who looks like that has to be cool.

She thanked her and got in. When she got in, a gust of wind blew her skirt up again. No tights, just a sexy synthetic panties.

Fine, then I just have to push that aside.

When she buckled up, I watched her. The seat belt ran between her tits and stretched the fabric of the blouse. Her tits stood out to the right and left of the strap like twice Mont Everest. Huge mountains with a deep valley.

My speed while driving was high, but just about acceptable. I was so looking forward to her little cunt. Was there someone in front of me? Had she made it herself? Had she ever seen a real cock? Touched one.

I almost hit the gate.

Why was there a gate here? Last year there was none. Last year with Angelika, a month before I met Roxana, we fucked right there. Was really cool.

But why is there a goal now?

4 The trap snaps shut.

The little girl unbuckled herself and came over to me, put her torso on mine, stuck her arm out of the window and rang the intercom. My face had firm firm tits. Tough. And the left wart bored into my chest. The place where they touched me burned hot.

"Yes please?" Came an ugly woman's voice from the set.

"It's me, Alessandra."

The gate opened and I drove inside. The little girl pointed to an empty parking lot. I headed for him as if in a trance.

"Do you want to come along? I'll show you where I'm sleeping. "

Sleep? Bed? Did she want to fuck? Geil, I'll come with you.

I nodded and followed her.

But we came into a large office after we had crossed the huge entrance hall and entered a new room .

was sitting behind a large desk an ugly old woman. Certainly those who had been on the intercom. Definitely already 80 or even older.

"Hello Alessandra."

"Hello Miss Margin."

Miss! Given the look, I'm not surprised that she didn't get a man, I thought amused.

"I see you brought someone with you."

Alessandra nodded.

"For your pleasure."

"Yes, Miss Margins. I am so horny. But nobody started. Except him. "

" Well, I'm happy for you. "

Bugger me. Permission to fuck? It was awesome.

The old box got up, went to a cupboard and came back with three glasses. She gave Alessandra and me a glass.

"Then to your good."

I drank hesitantly with them. Had I ended up in a children's pouf?

"Then show him your toys."

Alessandra put her glass on the desk, unbuttoned her blouse and showed me her gigantic tits. I raised a hand.

"Feel free to touch her. They are yours. "

I reached out and just when I could almost touch it the curtain fell on me.

5 First day

When I came to, my first thought was that I had been attacked. I couldn't move. At first I thought I was bound. But since I could move my head, I saw that I was lying on an X-shaped cross with all four of me stretched out. Not hanging, but lying.

Naked!

Fuck? If I should be allowed to fuck her now, it shot through my head. Funny that I still thought of the little cunt in this situation and not of danger. But those tits hovered in my mind's eye. They were really great. I waited for me to move again and for her to come in.

Uh, where was I actually here? I turned my head and saw only old rock faces. To the right and left of me a brick passage and behind my head also one. This "crypt?" Was illuminated by a few torches. Really spooky.

I lay there for a while, then I heard them coming. There were several people. First of all, a naked girl. Really cool. Alessandra! Now I also saw that she had no hair at the bottom of her cunt. The little horny pig.

She stood between my legs spread wide, looked at my long cock.

Why didn't it stand? Funny. Normally he would have, at the sight of the tits and the shaved cunt broken the neck.

"So I like you?"

"Yes," I wanted to say. But no sound came from my throat. So I just nodded.

"You want to fuck me?"

I nodded again, unable to use my voice.

"Push me in my pussy? In my ass? In my Fickschnauze? "

Again and again I nodded violently, in bright anticipation.

" Ever fucked a child like me. "

I shook my head.

"I would like to believe you," she said, her voice growing larger and screeching.

Did I see that correctly? Are there really wrinkles on her face? On the eyes? Now on her mouth too. The skin grew wrinkled. And at the same time it grew. To make a long story short, before my eyes she changed from a horny little girl to an old disgusting ugly smelly cunt. Worse looking than the old witch up in the office.

"Don't worry, you'll lick me more often than you 'd like."

Alessandra stepped back.

Did I hear and see correctly? Was I on an LSD trip?

What did I get to drink?

At the sign of Alessandra I started the others standing around us, piled up smoking bushes and leaves below me, the smoke cut my lungs, but still got enough air to breathe.

At first I didn't notice anything. But then I felt a twitch, as if my hair had been slowly pulled out. In the middle of the chest. But there was nobody around me. When it repeated itself several times and finally became uncomfortable, I looked at my chest. At first I didn't see anything. The feeling had now passed from the chest to the back, the thigh and the upper arms. And now I saw it. My hair pulled back into my skin with increasing speed. Wherever they grew, a pimple with a plug of pus formed under the tug. This contracted, burst and the pus poured over my skin. The beeping became a real fire. It became painful when it spread to the armpits, the pubic area and the sac region. Now it got so painful as if you stabbed my body with needles. I screamed as loud as I could as it spread across my face and upper lip. But no sound came from my wide open mouth. My voice was not there.

It must have taken hours before it finally subsided and then disappeared completely.

Some of the figures approached me and poured water over a body.

With boiling water!

My body screamed in pain! But not my mouth. No sound came from him.

The boiling water washed away the pus and poured itself onto the smoking bushes. There was a hissing steam that enveloped my body.

Then I felt a press on my head. An uncomfortable push.

I couldn't see it, but where my receding hairline was, and where my advanced bald head was, my scalp was bubbling. Where the desert had been for years, new roots formed under the skin. And not just there. The sparse hair growth on my head turned into a lush mane in minutes. When the hair sprouting from them pushed through the scalp, it was as if needles were pushed inside out. Initially uncomfortable, then unbearable.

In addition, there was this pull as they grew longer and longer. Another herb was thrown into the pile, which colored my hair red. Someone tied them up so they wouldn't hang in the still smoking bushes.

I don't know how long this took, then it stopped smoking.

The figures came closer and examined their work.

Suddenly the old Tusse, who had once been the horny Alessandra, came to me with a funnel. I pressed my lips together, my teeth.

At least that's what I thought.

But she opened my mouth as if it were a closet door. She put the funnel deep into my mouth and I expected the urge to vomit. But he didn't come. Just when I thought it would get into my stomach, it was over. She would pour 3 liters of a hideously smelly syrup into me. I almost thought I was suffocating, then it was over. With a jerk she pulled out the funnel. Looked at me with a smile with her stumps of teeth, the wart on her upper lip.

This is what the witch from Hansel and Gretel must have looked like.

Then a lightning struck me.

Fire burned in my head.

In my head?

Why in my head and not in my stomach?

But I didn't have time to think about it. My head seemed to burst. My eyes jumped out of the caves. I felt my teeth come out of bed. Little by little I spat it out. So I could do that again. Then my ears boomed. Like a ringing of bells, like the drum solo from Iron Butterfly and the big Japanese drums together, sometimes a thousand and amplified with the largest amplifier system in the world. My eardrum had to give up the ghost at any moment. Well, I couldn't hear well on the right anyway and a trinitus gave me a whistle day and night. But without hearing it was shit. And just as this swell subsided, a toothache flashed through me. All of my teeth that had remained in the years were outside, but it still hurt now. And not just just hurt. Imagine the worst toothache you have ever had. Multiplies that by 1000. And how many teeth does a person have? Exactly! Times the number of teeth and you can almost get to the pain I suffered.

I ran my tongue over my toothless mouth. I felt an elevation here and there. Then a tip that slowly drilled out of the gums. Then I recognized it.

I grew new teeth!

This realization was the only bright spot in the situation.

New teeth, instead of the 15 that had remained until then. When the pain subsided completely, I was amazed to hear the people around me clearly murmuring. So I heard better too!

The trinitus, the whistling was gone!

Startled, I opened my eyes, which I had closed all the time. I saw this old, young, girl, witch leaning over my face. From a distance I would have to put my glasses on to be able to recognize them. But I didn't need it. I saw her crystal clear and pin sharp less than 10 centimeters in front of me as she looked into my eyes, and nodded contentedly.

She went away. Everyone else too. I heard from the room to my left eating noises, glass blades. From the one on my right, the opposite. Farts, splashes, splashes and the sound of a water rinse.

However, from the room that lay behind my head, there were clear sounds of sex. "Deeper", "Tighter", "Leak faster", and so on.

I don't know how long I was there. Despite the excruciating pain, I found the result great.

All teeth back, ears OK, eyes too. Apparently I wouldn't have to shave anymore either.

I didn't know at that point that I would have to wake, dry and brush my mane much longer from now on.

6 Second day

A loud chime made my tormentors approach my cross again.

They piled up bushes again, but have not yet set fire to them. Then they poured scalding water on me again. Every nerve on my skin screamed. I hoped to pass out. But didn't happen. From the corner of my eye I saw how my skin, blistering, detached itself from the flesh. But where it detached, new, darker ones immediately formed. The pain, initially unbearable, increased a thousandfold.

For hours I lay on the cross screaming in pain.

Then I could feel it stop on the right ring finger, then on the big left toe, then on the left ear.

More and more places stopped hurting. Finally it was over. I saw a beautiful velvety skin. In terms of color, just like two or three weeks of Spain without sunburn. Internally satisfied with the result, I calmed down again. So far, despite the excruciating pain, I had only benefited.

But then they set the bushes on fire.

Oddly enough, the smoke didn't take my breath away. But the heat was unbearable.

Did they want to roast me? My body screamed for cooling. I heard my joints crack. My bones made grinding noises. My spine cracked. My head seemed to shrink. I had a headache.

Then I felt the cross slowly being lengthened on all four beams. At first I thought they wanted to stretch you. But my body wasn't tied down. So what was that about? Then I felt the pain in my fingers and toes. I prayed to die. It was the worst thing I had ever experienced. All the pain together, and multiplied by itself, was nowhere near that pain.

This must have gone on for hours.

Then the smoke subsided, as did the pain.

Finally it was over. I was lying on this cross and I didn't know what was happening to me.

7 Third day

The attendees again went out to eat in the room. Then in the other rooms.

After another loud chime rang, they all came to the cross again. They all nodded in agreement. Apparently they found my new exterior satisfactory.

The old woman came to me again and gave me a caustic brew through the funnel. My throat burned like fire, my stomach rebelled. But he kept everything inside.

Unfortunately.

Because what followed was horrible.

The pain of the previous torture tours combined was just a prick with a needle, which was followed by a trip through a meat grinder followed by an acid bath.

At first it started quite harmlessly.

I noticed that it started where I knew fat knots under my skin. They got warm, warmer, then really hot. But then it started in the legs, from there into my arms. When it started in my chest, I became terrified.

I had constrictions in my coronary arteries. Well, they had been stretched out with a wire mesh. But not everywhere. Would I have a heart attack now?

But then the torture started.

My eggs seemed to have been clamped in a vise that was slowly and relentlessly twisting. My cock burned like holding a blowtorch on it. The skin around my chest contracted and I got anxiety. I squinted down at myself as far as my immobility allowed, but I couldn't see any flames.

It became unbearable. I peeked down again to see expected flames. But when I looked down, I could see my nipples. Just the top. They stood stiff and firm in my perspective. They're still there, I thought with relief, but what about my cock? What about my eggs?

I felt like they were crushed in the vise. Completely useless. No longer needed.

I lay there for a long time, motionless, with my eyes closed. Surrendered me to this hell tour. Finally I squinted at myself again. My God, I saw my nipples, firm and hard erect, standing in the middle of a dark courtyard and:

skin!

Skin with meat underneath. Like with tits. With real tits!

Did my tits grow?

As often as the pain allowed me, I squinted down. And in the perspective, two huge boobs rose more and more. Long after the pain in her arms and legs subsided, only her chest and eggs hurt. I knew what was with my chest. They had turned into tits. And what kind of. They easily withstood a comparison with those of Alessandra. But my balls and my cock. When I was done here I would give the little cunt a fuck, whether with or without skin folds on the face.

Then the pain was gone.

Everything was gone!

No burning, no itching, no pulling. Nothing!

As if you just turned it off.

Another chime sounded.

8 awakening

Everyone present got rid of their cloaks. Underneath, old, ugly women emerged. Then the first turned into a young girl. 17, 18 years old. Then the second, 16? The third.

In this way girls were created, one more beautiful than the other. All with plenty of wood in front of the hut, shaved cunts up to the age of 25.

I looked at them one after the other .

My God! I could move my head!

I tried one hand.

You obeyed me!

The arm, the other arm. I pulled my legs up, could feel them. I swung myself into a sitting position without effort, dangling my legs.

My God, had I only dreamed all of this? Had drugs been involved? I jumped off the cross, looked at one girl after the other. Then I came to

Alessandra. I wanted that. I went up to her and she looked at my crotch. She was definitely looking expectantly at my cock.

How big it was. I was only a little taller than her!

Funny.

Then I thought of the cross. How could I have let my legs dangle? Why did I have to jump down? It wasn't that high after all. Why didn't I feel my sack when I walk and rock my cock? And why did I have this "overweight"?

Front!

I touched my chest.

Tits!

I grabbed my crotch.

A slit!

I looked at my arms.

Small, short!

My god, I was still on the trip!

"Alessandra! Take your little friend. And have a lot of fun with her. "

Alessandra pulled me by the arm. I was too stunned to fight back. On the other hand. If that was a trip, I would stick my cock in her. They fuck to the point of unconsciousness.

She led me up a small spiral staircase that I hadn't noticed before, through the large hall, then up the stairs to the first floor, down the long corridor, and on the walls hung pictures of old women, all standing by the cauldron or touching it , or sitting at a table with a high hat, books in front of them, some of them with a black bird or a black cat.

That's how I imagined the witches in fairy tales as a child.

When Alessandra opened the door to her room and we went in, I was hoping to wake up from this nightmare. When we entered a woman stood in the room and looked out of the window.

"I warned you!"

That was Roxana's voice!

She turned around.

Yes! It was.

"I warned you. You didn't want to listen to me."

"Roxana! What's going on here? "

" What should be going on here? "

"What drug did you give me? When I look at my breast, I see tits, when I touch my cock, I only feel a slit. "

" Isn't that normal in a girl? "

The last sentence hung over me like a sword of Damocles. It repeated booming in my head.

With a girl.

With a girl!

With a girl !!!

"What?"

"Didn't I tell you I'm a witch?"

"Yes, but."

"Of course you didn't believe it."

"No. Of course not. There are no witches. "

" Oh. Not? "

Alessandra nudged me with a bra in her hand.

"Dress up."

I laughed at her.

Then Alessandra hit me in the face.

A girl, not older than 18 wants to hit me, a grown man? We want to see that.

I raised my hand to the blow when it flashed from her hand and I flew across the room, lying there with an aching back.

"Get up!" She shouted at me.

"Get on you piece of dirt!"

I rose, trembling with anger.

"Alessandra, are you familiarizing her with the rules?"

"Yes mistress."

"Give her a nice name. It should become our flagship. "

" Yes. "

Then Roxana left the room and Alessandra buckled in front of her.

When she closed the door behind her and I could have sworn she hadn't touched the handle, Alessandra turned to look at her.

"From now on you will be called Veronique! Do you understand?"

I wanted to look up when she threw another flash out of her hand, which in turn threw me across the room.

But I didn't want to be beaten so easily.

But half an hour later I was whimpering like a little girl, and I was now, in a corner of the room, begging for her to stop.

Then she came to me.

I put my hands over my face in fear. But she tenderly took my hand and helped me get up. Then she stroked the bruises, the dents and scratches very gently. She spoke words that I did not understand. A pull went through the spots and the bruises were gone.

"Now get dressed," she said in a tender voice.

She held the bra out to me and scared I took it from her hand. When I had squeezed my breasts into the cups, she turned me around and closed it. She handed me a pair of panties, which I put on. For the first time I really noticed the weight of my breasts. They literally pulled me over when I got into my panties.

"Sit on the bed. I'll show you how to put on pantyhose. So far you have only undressed the girls. "

I sat down obediently and she showed me how to wind up a pair of pantyhose, put your foot in and then slowly walk up your leg. Only now did I notice that my fingernails had grown. Right They looked pretty on my hands.

But what was I thinking?

"And now the blouse."

She held out a blouse and I promptly misjudged my buttons. They were on the other, the left. Alessandra helped me. It was strange. But somehow I liked her touch.

"And now the skirt."

She handed me a part, which probably deserved the name "broad belt". It was very short and far. It just covered my bottom. But just now. Even when walking normally, the skirt wiggled back and forth on my buttocks so that everyone who looked could see my panties.

"And now the shoes."

My God! They had heels. Not exactly stiletto heels. But 6 or 7 centimeters high and narrow. And when I put them on, Alessandra pulled me to the mirror.

My god I have nice long legs. The panties will look out with every step. And my breasts. Just a poem. And how they felt.

I couldn't get enough of my new exterior.

"Sit down on the bed."

I sat down with Alessandra next to me.

And then she explained the rules to me.

Once a year I have to bring a man here. One who really wants to fuck me.

How I do it and whether I do leave it to me beforehand, that would be up to me. The only

thing that is important is that he follow me here. Then this house could read my body as much as it is now. If I can't do it, I would age by a year.

"You'll think I'm 17:18 now, what the hell. But before you know it you're 21st then 30th then 50th then 100th And at some point it's too late and you'll die. "

" Alessandra? "

"Yes darling?"

"How old are you? I really mean."

"122."

I had to swallow.

"And one more thing. As soon as you are here in the house, you are my slave. You will do what I say. During the day, like everyone else, you will go to school here. You will learn everything you can All the magic you need. At night you are only there for me. You will see that if you study hard and do it well, you will have it well.

9 The hunt for life

Alessandra brought me down to the dining room. Everyone seemed to like my exterior. And frankly, I felt very comfortable in this girl's body. Especially since I had gotten rid of my frailties. And my appearance would have made me crazy earlier. I would have thrown myself into the bushes and nibbled.

I sat down anxiously next to Alessandra at the table. At first I thought reluctantly what witches eat.

Rats, spiders, snakes and such.

Fortunately, you ate normal dishes. The meal was done with a lot of talk. Very often Alessandra was asked if she could "borrow" me from another witch for the night.

But Alessandra said no .

About an hour later the table was picked up and Alessandra led me to our room. Only now did I realize that there was only one broad bed there.

"Do we sleep together in bed?" I asked her.

"Only if you are good. You will sunbathe in the basement."

She started to undress and indicated to me to do the same. Within a few minutes we were both naked in the room. She pulled me to the bed and lay down.

"Do it to me. But do it well, bask! "

This bask was so powerful that I immediately thought of the basement and imagined the most terrible things down there.

I still knew how to melt a woman with hands and tongue. But none of it seemed right. Finally I sat crying on the bed while Alessandra scolded me.

Stupid child, little idea of ??her own body, stupid bitch, and much more she threw at my head.

Finally she explained to me what I had to do and how.

As a man, I had always made sure to excite my partner quickly, and she showed me how it was done very slowly and gradually. And luckily I learned quickly. I never had to go to the basement. Even more.

She showed me how it was with me a few days later. And my first orgasm as a girl was insane. Had I tried to imagine him earlier, it couldn't match what really happened to me.

In the following weeks and months I learned everything I needed to know as a little witch until afternoon. Then Alessandra taught me everything I needed to know as a girl. Make up, hairdressing, clothes. Everything I needed to know for my life. And so I was well prepared when I went "hunting" 11 months later. It only took 12 minutes, then I had a young man on the fishing rod who followed me willingly, hoping to fuck a young horny girl .

I do not want to reproduce what happened to him here. So much can be said that he never walked among the living again.

That was 67 years ago. I got one every year and kept my youth.

I also saw Roxana again. I was even allowed to sleep with her very often. But without my cock. I missed it less and less over time. Life as a girl is wonderful. And the life of a witch even more.

After 4 years I even visited my friend Heinz and his wife Klaudia. At first he didn't want to believe me. However, when I told him our secrets from school, he calmed down. Finally, he believed me. Last but not least, his wife Klaudia was the deciding factor when she brought him to us 5 years later.

Klaus, today he is called Cordula, or rather she is my best friend.

But Alessandra is my lover.

The End.

My friend Marlies

When I was 18 I had a friend, Marlies, the same age. It was of course the "big love", but - that's how it was back then - besides holding hands, smooching, looking into the blouse and even stroking your hands between your thighs, there was nothing else - the fear of unwanted pregnancy and At that time we were still sitting on the back of our necks, the parents

lived a little outside in the settlement, we had been eating ice cream in the city and I took the tram to the terminus where she had to change to the bus, but the bus The direction of the settlement was already gone, the next was only in three quarters of an hour. "Come on," I said, "we're going on foot, I'll take you home. Then you will be home earlier than waiting for the next bus. "

We ran through the allotments on the outskirts of the city and - as is usual with a couple in love - constantly interrupted our way with smooching, our hands more under our skirts and pants than we did ourselves. We groaned and swore at love first houses of the settlement. Suddenly Marlies stopped, nudged me from the side and said: "Wait a minute, I have to pee!" On the way behind a blackberry hedge she was already lifting with a loud "Huhu!" the skirt, so that I could see her red-dotted panties, which contained an exciting butt. I was really excited by the fumbling on the way home, but now the pants were really tight. Alone the idea of ??how she would crouch behind the hedge, without panties and with her skirt rolled up,

Grinning, Marlies came back to me on the way, hands behind his back. "I have something for you," she said softly, "you'll like that and I'll give it to you!" She pulled out the briefs with the red dots behind her back and handed them to me. "He got a few drops of excitement when I pulled him down, but I don't think that will bother you." I stared in fascination at the soaking wet part in my hand - from "a few drops" - until Marlies woke me up from my dreams. "Come on, just take me to the next street corner, my parents don't have to see everything." After a long goodbye kiss we parted there, I stood there with the wet, fragrant ball in my hand, I couldn't do it well Pocket.

My path led me back through the allotments and I was constantly sniffing Marlies' pissy panties. At the blackberry hedge I looked around to see if no one was watching me, then I opened my pants and wrapped my pissed panties around my stiff cock. I only had to jerk off briefly, then the juice shot into the wet cloth. I hadn't hosed so hard for a long time.

We quickly realized that we had a common hobby, which made our connection a very special one. We dealt with the topic of "water sports & pee" more openly, but since we both still lived at home, these games mostly took place outdoors - a piss-soaked sheet has to be explained to parents first.

So, we were on vacation and I went to the Rhine with Marlies. We had told her parents that we would go to the swimming pool and meet friends, but it was quieter for a couple in love on the banks of the Rhine. We looked for a quiet spot in the tall grass, rolled out the towels and threw the clothes over the moped - I didn't have a car at the time - we had already put on our bathing suit at home. "The tea from breakfast wants to get out," said Marlies and took two steps to the side. Marlies always peed standing and not crouching, even in the pool in the back corner of the fence. So she stood with her legs apart in the grass, her back turned to me and the loose-fitting bikini bottoms made of red fabric pulled between the legs to the side.

But another sight captivated me. By pulling on the gusset, the panties were pulled back a little so that a part of the gap between the white buttocks was visible. "Good idea," I said, "I have to!" I walked the two steps over to her, but stopped behind her, pushed my swimming trunks down, took my cock out and pissed off: Exactly in the exciting crack above the panties. A dark line immediately formed on the red fabric, which quickly became wider and longer. I had surprised Marlies because she winced briefly. "You're a sow - but a dear one!" She leaned over and stretched her butt towards me. I now steered the tail with my hand and let the warm jet wander over the two buttocks until all the bikini bottoms were soaked.

When she noticed that the warm tide was drying up with me, she slowly turned and took her hand out of her crotch. Here, too, the trousers were dark, her thick pubic hair was visible under the wet fabric, her two legs glistened damp. "Look at me, what should I do now?" She asked with mock accusation. "Take off and let it dry in the sun!" I grinned and stowed my tail in my swimming trunks. "I would like that!" She said and grinned back. I would have really liked it because I had seen her naked a few times while changing clothes and the sight of her densely hairy black triangle was enough for me as a wank template for weeks. "I got it ", she said," I just lie down on your towel with your wet pants and you lie on mine. Punishment is needed!"

Five minutes later she suddenly sat up next to me and sat on my chest. "So you know how cold such a wet fabric is," she said, slowly starting to slide back and forth on my chest and belly, leaving a damp trail. She supported herself with both hands and I could hold her small breasts in the Seeing the bikini hanging - a sight to behold, she slowly slid deeper until she was sitting on the semi-rigid in my swimming trunks. Suddenly it got warm there, she peed through my bikini onto my swimming trunks, from where it ran between my legs into the towel "I stopped earlier and saved something for you," she said softly and began to slide back and forth. "You are a sow - but also a love," I said and gave her a kiss, I squeezed a short jet out of the almost empty bladder, which in this position sprayed me almost up to my neck. Marlies gently rubbed the juice on my chest with my hand. "As you said: just let it dry in the sun!", She laughed and rolled back onto the towel. I squeezed a short jet out of the almost empty bladder, which in this position sprayed me almost up to my neck. Marlies gently rubbed the juice on my chest with my hand. "As you said: just let it dry in the sun!", She laughed and rolled back onto the towel.

The End.

The advertisement

Unfortunately, I had my first sexual experience with another woman at the age of 34, so now about 2 years ago.

Had I known how wonderful passionate sex with a woman can be, I would have tried it earlier.

It all started with a newspaper advertisement.

I had just divorced my ex-husband in six months. We had gotten apart because we both worked a lot and one day my husband confessed to me that he was in love with another woman and so it came to a separation.

Basically, I wasn't really angry with him, it hadn't worked properly in bed for a long time and so it was probably better that way.

Half a year later, I read the newspaper in the morning in my eat-in kitchen before work.

I am a very successful interior designer and on this sunny spring morning I didn't have a customer appointment until 10:30 a.m., so I could enjoy my breakfast in peace.

I don't know if it was because I hadn't had proper sex for more than half a year or if it was just boredom. This morning I also read the personals, which I hardly ever do otherwise.

Under the heading "He is looking for you" I noticed another category "She is looking for her" with only one advertisement. I got curious and read:

"19 year old student is looking for a mature woman to live out their shared fantasies. Letters under code 6969"

When I read that, it hit me like a blow.

I read the ad a second time.

I could hardly believe it, when a 19 year old girl was looking for an older woman to go wild with her!

At this point I should perhaps mention that the idea of ??having sex with a woman has turned me on for years.

It started when I was watching porn with my (now ex-) husband to bring a little momentum to our sex life. Of course, almost every one of these porn also had scenes in which two or more women were having sex with each other. Presumably men like that - my ex-husband, too, by the way.

In any case, to my own amazement, I found that these lesbian scenes always turned me on. And when I masturbated, I imagined more and more that I was doing it with a woman.

After I was divorced, I actually even ordered pure lesbian porn on DVD over the Internet. And frankly, that has been my absolute favorite porn lately.

The scenes in which two women lick each other's wet pussies and then rub their hot pussies against each other always made me incredibly horny, and mostly it didn't take long for me to have a violent orgasm. But until then I had never thought of putting these fantasies into practice.

But now I was confronted with it.

I read the ad out loud a third time.

My imagination went crazy.

Scenes in which a 19-year-old licked my wet pussy, how I stroked her young cunt and fucked her with my fingers, how we rub our slick cunts to the point of ecstasy and similar messes shot through my head and I felt like I always did got wet between my legs.

Shocked by my own lustful thoughts, I pouted myself and wondered if I was completely nuts now or if I just hadn't had sex for too long.

I put the newspaper aside and realized that I had to start going to work.

But I couldn't get this ad out of my head all day.

When I finally got home in the evening, my first glance was at the newspaper, which was still open on the kitchen table.

I read the ad again:

"A 19-year-old student is looking for a more mature woman to live out their shared fantasies. Letters under box 6969"

With a sigh I put the newspaper aside.

Since I had a meeting with a customer and his architect on a construction site in the afternoon and it was quite dusty there, I wanted to take a shower quickly.

I undressed in the bathroom. When I stood so naked in front of the mirror, I looked at my body and wondered if a 19-year-old girl could take pleasure in me.

I have short blonde hair and blue eyes. Since I attended a spinning class twice a week in the gym, I was still in great shape for my age. My butt was still quite crunchy and my toned thighs showed little signs of cellulite. But I was particularly proud of my breasts, which were not too big and not too small and gravity had hardly left any traces. My nipples were already standing out slightly excited. I always shaved my pussy completely bald before my fitness training. I loved not only the soft feeling but also the wonderful sight of a bald shaved cunt! I had quite large labia and a fairly large clit that was already sticking out of her hiding place, I noticed.

The whole day I had been thinking about the 19 year old student and so I was really horny and pretty wet!

I climbed into the hot shower and started to soap myself with relish. My hands wandered over my hot body and my thoughts back to the advertisement and the 19 year old girl.

I let my imagination run wild and imagined stroking and kissing her young, tight body, sucking on her stiff nipples and finally shoving my tongue into her wet cunt and tasting her hot cunt juice.

Of course, my hand had long been between my legs and stroked my rock-hard clit with rapid back and forth movements, while my other hand massaged my breasts.

I imagined myself watching her relishly lick my wet pleasure cleft and suck on my stiff clit. At the thought of rubbing my wet cunt on hers, I finally got into an incredibly violent orgasm. Despite the running shower, I felt my cunt juice running down my hand and the inside of my thighs as my body went through one pleasure wave after another.

Wow, that was really hard!

And from that moment on I knew what I had to do!

After I finished showering, drying myself, and getting dressed in something comfortable, I took a notepad from my desk in the bedroom and the newspaper from the kitchen and sat down with a glass of wine in the living room and began to write a letter with trembling hands:

" Dear strangers,

I read your ad in the newspaper ... "

The End.